The Big Pancake

by Susan Gates

illustrated by Alan Rogers

The cook made a big pancake.

'It looks good,' he said.

'It's the biggest pancake I have ever seen!'

But the pancake jumped out of the pan and rolled away.

'Come back,' shouted the cook.

The big pancake did not come back.

'The cook wants to eat me,' said the pancake.

It rolled faster and faster.

The pancake came to a house.
'Help me!' shouted a lady.

'Jump!' shouted the big pancake.
'I'll catch you!'

The pancake rolled on.

The cook and the lady ran after the pancake.
'They want to eat me,' the pancake said.
The pancake came to a road.

'Help!' shouted a boy.
'My goats will fall into the big hole!'

'I can help you!' said the pancake.

The pancake rolled on.

The cook and the lady and the boy ran after the pancake.

The pancake came to a river.
'Help!' shouted a little girl. 'She can't swim!'

The pancake came to a hill.

'I can't roll up a hill,' said the pancake.

'I am too tired.

You will just have to eat me.'

'You helped the lady and the boy and the little girl,' said the cook.

'We want to say thank you.'

'Hurray for the big pancake!' they all shouted.

Blue band

The Big Pancake — Susan Gates
Teaching notes written by Sue Bodman and Glen Franklin

Using this book

Developing reading comprehension
This reworking of a traditional tale focuses on a cook who gives chase to his pancake. Along the way, the pancake helps a series of characters. They all give chase, too. The tale takes a change of direction as it becomes clear that they do not want to eat it, but say thank you.

Grammar and sentence structure
- Speech is sustained over more than one utterance.
- Longer sentences are created by adding characters to the repeated sequence.

Word meaning and spelling
- Use of comparatives *faster*, *biggest*.
- Decoding new and unfamiliar words, supported by context and meaning.
- Opportunity to rehearse automatic, fast recognition of high-frequency words.

Curriculum links
Science – In this story, the pancake is able to use his material properties to help people: it breaks the lady's fall and allows her to bounce; it floats; it can stick over a hole. Explore household materials to see which of the situations they would be useful in, if any.

Food Technology – Follow some recipes to make types of pancake. Which do the children prefer?

Learning Outcomes
Children can:
- solve unfamiliar words using print information and understanding of the text
- sustain accurate reading over a greater number of lines of text on a page
- comment on events, characters, and ideas, making imaginative links to their own experience.

A guided reading lesson

Book Introduction
Give each child a copy of the book. Read the title and the blurb with them. Then say: *The cook made the big pancake*. Ask the children to suggest why lots of people might run after the pancake.

Orientation
Do you know any other stories like this, where lots of people join in to chase after something? If they have read the Gingerbread Man briefly reprise the plot to get the idea of characters joining the chase

Give a brief overview of the story, using the same verb tense as used in the book. *In this book, the cook made a big pancake. But it jumped out of the pan and ran away. Let's see where it runs and if the cook ever caught it.*

Preparation
Pages 2 and 3: Support use of comparative language by saying; *Wow, that pancake is big. It's much bigger than the cook's usual frying pan.* Guide the children to notice that as the cook tossed it, it jumped out of the pan. Ask the children to suggest how it moved; after some suggestions take them to the word 'rolled' and ask the children to read slowly across the word to solve it.

Pages 4 and 5: Point out 'faster and faster'; Ask: *why is the pancake getting faster and faster?* Draw attention to the repeated sentence pattern, 'The cook wants to eat me'. Ask: *What do you think will happen next?*